BLAME NOT THE CHILD

(The story of growing up in the Eastern part of Nigeria, during the ill-fated Biafran Republic).

Alozie I. Ikonne

Order this book online at www.trafford.com
or email orders@trafford.com

Most Trafford titles are also available at major online book retailers.

Printed in Victoria, BC, Canada.

ISBN: 978-1-4269-1141-5 (soft)
ISBN: 978-1-4269-1142-2 (hard)

*Our mission is to efficiently provide the world's finest, most comprehensive book publishing
service, enabling every author to experience success. To find out how to publish your
book, your way, and have it available worldwide, visit us online at www.trafford.com*

Trafford rev. 12/03/2009

www.trafford.com

North America & international
toll-free: 1 888 232 4444 (USA & Canada)
phone: 250 383 6864 ♦ fax: 812 355 4082

DEDICATION

To my father and mother, Israel (late) and Elinah Ikonne; who defied all odds to raise and nurture an ideal home that gave me the right start in life.

ACKNOWLEDGEMENT

I owe a debt of gratitude to many people who in practise and learning have been wonderfully used of God to shape and encourage me in this life.

First, I thank my father and mother who kept faith with the family values during the Civil War, and sacrificed everything to ensure that the children did not die of starvation. My oldest brother's wife, **Lady Grace Ikonne,** whose services at the Red Cross helped to provide the needed provisions for a kwashiorkor- free life during the war. My older brother, **Engr. Amadi A. Ikonne,** who in the absence of any vehicle carried our family belongings on his head during our many days of trekking from place to place.

My oldest brother, **Elder Godwin Ikonne** who planted the seed of seeking for knowledge and intellectual development. You are indeed a rare gem. I thank my lovely wife and children for the time they granted me to be with the computer in the course of writing. Thank you so much for your sacrifice.

My special thanks go to **Professor Anthony I. Nwabughuogu** of the Abia State University, who read the initial manuscript, and also wrote the foreword to this book. The Management and Staff of **Cinoryz World Services Owerri,** which designed the cover and setting of the book for publication.

Finally, to my Publishing Consultant, **Nancy Patino Marin** of the **Trafford Publishing Company** for her useful advice in the course of producing this book. God bless you.

Contents

FOREWORD

Blame Not The Child has attempted to bring together in one book, and from a satirical and philosophical focus, very pertinent reflections on the Nigerian Civil War. These reflections centre on two key issues both of which have escaped detailed treatment in existing literature on the Nigerian Civil War.

These are: the lasting effect of the civil war on the psyche of those children who were raised up in the defunct Republic of Biafra and the broader effect of the civil war on the processes of nation building in Nigeria.

The author has used his personal experiences as one who grew up in the period of the Nigerian

Civil war to propound a hypothesis, which should be tested through further research, that "children who grow up under war situations are likely to develop deviant and defiant attitudes later on in life."

The trauma which children go through during periods of war, the shells which fall on their houses, dislocation of the family system, the destruction of infrastructure as well as the society's mechanism for conflict resolution; and the collapse of the value systems of the people make the development of the new attitudes of defiance and deviance in children inevitable when they grow up. It is therefore against this background that the attitudes of today's youth must be understood.

The author goes on to establish the linkage between the civil war, and the wider problems of nation building in Nigeria. According to him, the immediate post-war experiences of the youth exacerbated the negative opinions they held for the nation during the war.

The failure of the Federal Government to satisfactorily fulfil its promise of reconciliation, reconstruction and rehabilitation created a sense of disillusionment among the youth of the defunct Biafra, causing them to migrate in large numbers to other parts of Nigeria, in search of better life.

This increased competition, albeit on unequal basis, for the resources of the Nigerian State and thus, intensified ethnic cleavages. Ethnicity bred the culture of violence, marginalization, intense suspicion and the penchant to "wait for the rations from the purse" rather than engage in productive ventures. Nation building has suffered as a result.

The author offers useful and practical recommendations that will, if implemented, restore hope and confidence in the Nigerian project, and move the country to greater heights.

Blame Not The Child is strongly recommended to the youth and Governments of this country, and to all those who wish the Nigerian nation-state to succeed. It is also useful to other African Governments which have had or are experiencing civil wars in their countries.

Professor Anthony I. Nwabughuogu
Abia State University,
Uturu, Abia State; Nigeria.
December, 2008

INTRODUCTION

The night was unusually long as the desire for a new day was all the people wanted. For a few years, there had been the desire for a change of leadership from the Oyibos to the indigenous people. Many meetings and conferences had been held to persuade the Colonial masters to pack their bags and baggage and leave for their homelands.

After what looked like an impossible situation, at last; the Colonial masters were ready to cede their authority over the Niger Area to the indigenous politicians. The night preceding the transfer of authority from master to servant was embraced with all enthusiasm. At last, the day of independence was about to replace the Empire day of the Colonial masters.

The British Union Jack was about to be replaced with the Green White Green of the new nation Nigeria. As that glorious first day of October in 1960 was ushered in, the nation and the people erupted in a spontaneous feeling of ecstasy on that sunny day that would turn the fortunes of the country and people around. H-a-p-p-y I-n-d-e-p-e-n-d-e-n-c-e rang and resonated throughout the length and breadth of the new nation. Politicians and local chiefs patted each other on the back for a feat they thought would take Nigeria from the dark forest to a golden state where everyone would live in paradise.

The departure of the British and their cousins left leadership gaps in the life of the new independent country. The local leaders, who forgot their tribal marks and personal interests to unite against the British and their cohorts, suddenly re-invented their trademarks. The struggle for control of political power and patronage became intensified.

People who fought a common foe a few years ago started to turn their ammunition against those who happened to come outside of their ethnic homeland. The acrimony and other diversionary schemes distracted the new political lords from pursuing the business of statecraft and national cohesion. 'The centre could no longer hold'. Every effort geared towards nation building was diverted to ethnic push up.

The post-colonial leadership of Nigeria became deceitful in major parameters of governance. With the lip, the leaders were shouting one nation, one destiny, but in their heart of hearts, every leader was working towards entrenching their own ethnic interests above the others. To outshine one another, political office that was supposed to be an avenue for selfless service, became a circuit show in hypocrisy and vanities.

Much energy was expended on building personal empires and personalisation of offices. Praise singing, nepotism and an unbridled corruption became the order of the day. With each passing day, less effort was geared towards national development.

In about six years, ominous signs started appearing on the structure of governance. Politics became increasingly brute and destructive. The little order the British left behind for the good governance of society became increasingly eroded. There was no more civilised and enlightened ways of doing business in the Nigerian society.

Elections were no more conducted within the framework of the prevailing laws. Thuggery and rigging became entrenched in the electoral culture, resulting in the loss of confidence in the sanctity of the ballot box. Might became right, and the nation was increasingly tilting towards a failed state.

It was at this point of near entropy that the Armed Forces of the Federal Republic of Nigeria struck and sacked the Constitutional Government. With the politicians sidelined, the new set of military rulers who were obviously not trained for governance drove the nation into deeper waters. It became a game of fists and wits as one group of soldiers were working to upstage one another.

Consequently, at this point coups and counter coups entered the political process. With the national cohesion gone, and soldiers giving more allegiance to their geographical and tribal blocks, the stage was then set for the attendant social upheaval that culminated to the Nigerian civil war.

This book is neither the history of the war, nor a chronicle of that unfortunate event that has marred the progress of this great nation. In the main, it is a satire on the dangers of human error and judgment, and the ugly consequences on the social contract between people. The characters in this story do not represent some of our illustrious leaders.

The story is the author's experience of growing up in Eastern Nigeria during the Civil war as a boy, and what I feel is the problem of the people of Nigeria especially the old Eastern Region. However, strategic places that contributed to the outcome of the War would be mentioned (though in reverse order). Let the reader not judge the book from the standpoint of a historian. This is simply a literary work, and no other meaning and reading are intended.

Each time fathers, mothers, leaders and adults fail in their God-given roles of setting and shaping the norms of society, the outcome impacts negatively on their children. Children would always live what they see. If they see the right standards or patterns, they follow those patterns. On the other hand, if the wrong things were placed before the children, trying to convince them otherwise would be like forcing the river to flow towards the mountain.

Welcome to the story, as you will soon discover why you should BLAME NOT THE CHILD.

Alozie Israel Ikonne
August 2007

"Any country that divides itself into groups which fight each other will not last very long; a family divided against itself falls apart."

Luke 11:17 (Holy Bible)

CHAPTER 1
WHEN IDEAS MATURE

There are popular sayings that wherever you may be, always remember that home is home. It all started as a pet idea that preserving the cultural and religious ideas of Elu is the best thing that could ever happen to the people. Every son and daughter of Elu is told that the people from Ala are distinct from him or her, and should not be allowed to break their cultural identity.

To some extent, the emergent leaders of Elu made it a point of duty to let their Ala brothers know that if every person keeps to his or her geographic location, that it was not a bad idea after all.

When this suggestion was made, the departing Oyinbos warned the Elu people not to toy with the idea of asking their Ala brothers to go their separate ways. They reasoned that unity is strength, and that the weakness of one part would be complimented by the strength of the other. The leaders of Elu accepted this time-tested counsel of the Oyibos until another argument erupted between the two people of Elu and Ala.

This time around, there had been series of upheavals between the people of Elu and their Ala brothers who live in the land of Elu. The trouble started over what the people of Ala did to their Elu brothers in the time past, which the Ala people thought their Elu brothers had forgiven them.

The trouble became so pronounced that people of Ala who were making their living in the land of Elu became objects of mob attacks.

BLAME NOT THE CHILD

Although well meaning people from the land of Elu condemned the attacks of the mob on their Ala brothers, nonetheless the attacks continued until unbearable proportions.

When the efforts of the leaders of Elu could not prevent the people from killing their brothers from Ala, the leaders of the Ala people issued a threat that the people of Elu should be held responsible for what happened to the unity of the two people of Elu and Ala.

The People of Ala also stated that since the people of Elu had been toying with the idea of each people going their separate ways, any further attacks on the people of Ala would mean that the idea of each people going their separate ways would be implemented without further delay. The people of Elu ignored that warning and continued to allow miscreants to maim and kill their Ala brothers.

At this point, the leaders of Ala announced to their Elu brothers that they had gone their separate ways. Some of the vocal voices that said that there was no basis for the unity of Elu and Ala suddenly made a u-turn and told their

Ala brothers that it was wrong for them to leave the union.

When it became apparent that each of the two blocks (Elu and Ala), were maintaining their positions, it was suggested by the leader of their distant cousin Anagh that the leaders of Elu and Ala should come to their country for amicable settlement.

The leaders of Elu and Ala accepted the offer from the people of Anagh. They went to the land of Anagh and settled at the city of Iruba where they held extensive deliberations and consultations. At the close of the meeting, the leaders of Elu and Ala hugged and posed for photographs. At last, peace had returned to the land of Elu and Ala, so it was thought.

Most times, people have some 'secret' or pet fancies of how things should be done their own way. This obsession to put one's view point through may lead to the pushing of personal ideas into corporate beliefs.

When the leaders of Elu returned to their land, every agreement they entered into with the leaders of Ala were out rightly repudiated. There was a stalemate as the basis of the agreement the two groups entered was no more binding. The two groups started searching for soft ground for landing, but would they find any?

"Conscience is an open wound, only truth can heal it"

- Uthman dan Fodio (1754-1817)

CHAPTER 2

THE ELDERS HAVE RETURNED

The much-trumpeted Iruba Accord that the two groups: Elu and Ala jointly signed started having some hiccups as soon as the two groups returned from the city of Iruba. Some of the elders on the side of Elu started questioning the veracity and wisdom of their own leaders in agreeing to append their signatures to a document they did not understand the whole implications.

With much pressure coming from various interest groups against the idea of signing the accord, it was a matter of time before the much trumpeted agreement would collapse. It did not take long before discordant tunes started coming from the camp of the people of Elu. Agitations emerged from influential quarters that the whole idea of the Iruba Accord should be rejected.

While the people of Elu were shifting their positions and commitments, their brothers from the land of Ala were equally holding consultations among themselves on possible reaction should the people of Elu go contrary to the agreement they willingly entered into with their Ala brothers. While the two sides to the dispute were strategising on how to gain advantage over the other, no one imagined the implication on the people.

When it became obvious that the Iruba Accord was no more going to stand, the leaders of Ala people quickly gathered in one of their cities called Araiha and proclaimed what is known as Araiha Declaration. This declaration authorised the leaders to have self-government and seek for the well being of all the people within the country of Ala.

This action of the leaders of Ala did not go down well with the leaders of Elu and their Ndida western cousins. Together, a task force was formed and mandated to go and bring back the leaders and people of Ala back to the country of Niger Area. While the leaders of Ala saw it as a challenge to prove that rejected people should not reject themselves, it wasn't long before some cracks appeared among the leadership of Ala.

Lack of agreement and subsequent back stabbing of one another became the order of the day. Any house divided against itself will ultimately collapse. It is an accepted fact in sea voyage that in moments of tempest, the easiest way to sink a ship is to appoint two captains at the same time.

No nation, people or family ever makes progress without a leader. In the final analysis, everything rises and falls at the feet of leadership. When elders fail in their God given duties and disagree; the outcome impacts greatly on their children.

The people of Elu were mobilising for war against the people of Ala with total agreement. On the other hand, the elders of Ala seemed not to know exactly who their real enemies were. Some leaders of Ala did not flow with their main leader, and subsequently, precious time and energy were expended on finding out who were genuine and who were saboteurs among the leadership.

With a full-blown war between the people of Elu and Ala, heroes and villains were created. Those who supported every step to hold on in the midst of economic blockade and hardship were celebrated as the real heroes. Those who seemed to surrender their pride and accept the terms of the opponents were labelled villains.

As the war was raging on, which was altogether fought on the very soils of the Ala people, unimagined calamities became the order of the day. Bombs and missiles rapidly destroyed social infrastructure. Food, salt and other means of survival were prevented from reaching to the nooks and crannies of the land of Ala.

The land of Ala had become the theatre of war and the people must bear the brunt of the conflict. War any day and time may be justified, but strategy is always better than strength. The people of Ala had to either survive the war, or survive the peace. But would they?

"The parents ate the sour grapes, But the children got the sour taste."

- (Ezekiel 18:2, Holy Bible)

CHAPTER 3
CHILD OF CIRCUMSTANCE

Ezeoha was born as a post independence child. Actually, he was born a few months before the republican birthday of the young nation Niger Area. He was growing up as one of the future leaders of the young nation in his rural village of Umueke. Everything was going on fine for Ezeoha and his peers in their sleepy village. There was sufficient food to eat and to share with neighbours. The people of Umueke were predominantly peasant farmers who enjoyed a measure of communal life.

The Local Authority School (LA School) in the village was just established to cater for the increasing desire of the village children to have access to western education. Ezeoha was one of the children in the village that showed signs of going to have western education.

One day, Ezeoha watched his father read his Bible in their local language, the father told him that one day, and he would enrol him at the LA school so that he would be an educated person and speak English like the Oyibos.

Ezeoha was growing up with the thought that one day he would be in school and learn like others. Every effort was therefore made by Ezeoha to be an obedient boy so as to encourage the father to send him to school. When Ezeoha was past five years, he was preparing his mind to begin his schooling career in January after the next Christmas.

One Sunday, after Church service, information was circulated that the war between the people of Elu and Ala was taking a different dimension. To make matters worse, Ezeoha and his mother came back from the farm the next Tuesday evening to find too many people in their village.

Most of the strangers were carrying basins, pots, mats and other household items. Some were speaking dialects that were strange to the one Ezeoha and his people spoke. They gathered at the village square and passed the night there.

The following Wednesday, more and more people trooped into the same village, telling stories of woes and sufferings. The village gong was sounded and all the adult males were summoned to brainstorm over the sudden influx of people to the village and the way out of the situation. Since children were not allowed to sit together with the elders, they were permitted to stay away and watch proceedings.

One of the refugees (as they were fondly called), who happened to be educated, told the story of how the soldiers from the land of Elu, invaded the Port city of Ala which was its gateway to the Atlantic Ocean and captured it. Having taken control of the Port City, the soldiers of Elu imposed naval blockade over the people of Ala.

With the only access route to the sea blocked, the people of Ala were then landlocked.

The surrounding towns and villages around the Port City came under heavy artillery and air bombardment. As the sides to the war were trying to have the upper hand, women and children were displaced. As the war was ragging, the people of Elu were having the upper hand because their cousins from the land of Ndida joined them to fight the people of Ala. More fighting led to the displacement of more people and there appeared to be no end in sight.

When the soldiers from the land of Elu eventually took the commercial town of Aba in the land of Ala, many more people had to migrate northwards. By this time, no one was talking of going to school. As many more people were displaced, the village halls were no more able to take the number of displaced people. Individual compounds were opened to accommodate the distressed and displaced people.

The sleepy village of Umueke was no longer the same. It had turned to a busy place in both the nights and the day. Since there was no electricity, the bush lanterns became the source of illumination. More people had to be deployed to the farms to take care of additional mouths to be fed.

Life was a sort of mixed grill, as everyone was forced by the circumstance to live a communal life. There was no more privacy, either in the rooms or outside. The trees, shades and bushes became places of habitation, depending on the daily circumstance.

The years 1967-1970 were years that the people of Ala would never forget easily. Everything was under serious threat. Infrastructure had been destroyed and the available resources were no more able to cope with level of the raging war. Transport systems had packed up due to infrastructure damage or lack of fuel to power engines. The educational system had collapsed because pupils and students were advised to stay indoors to avoid being killed by bombs and missiles.

The people of Ala deployed all available human and material resources to prosecute the war. This led to food shortages and the attendant hunger. The economic blockade prevented the people of Ala from importing food, medicine and other raw materials for production. Because of hunger and malnutrition, people were dying like flies.

Since the men had been drafted to the war fronts, only women and children were left to produce food for all. Women and children who did not die of hunger, suffered from severe malnutrition often described as kwashiorkor.

The dream of going to school, which Ezeoha had nursed, started fading away as each week; the very LA school playground was turned to a food-rationing centre. All the children from the village of Umueke and other adjoining places would come with their bowls to collect what was usually referred to as 'blended'. The so-called blended was simply cornmeal which was either prepared there at the field, or shared for the people to prepare at home.

The Red Cross and other agencies that assisted in alleviating the sufferings of the people of Ala provided the food centres. Because of the acute shortage of salt, fishes laced with salt were provided as compliment to the salt needs of the people. Vitamin supplements were packed in little containers and shared among the people.

BLAME NOT THE CHILD

Life in the nation of Ala had become a different thing to the people. All dreams, visions and goals set by both individuals and communities were put on hold. The village cohesion and other community bonds were increasingly subjected to external influences.

What started as a rare occurrence gradually began to be the routine experience. Daily, people woke up to dodge shells and mortar that were flying all over the place. Everyone went round the village with pieces of leaves covering the head.

The village of Umueke was no more the same, as air raids, with possible bombs became the order of the day. Languages like, 'take cover, take cover' were heard each time the Mig and Alpha jet fighters used by the people of Elu flew over the territory of Ala.

Ezeoha and other young people in the village of Umueke faced the daily routine of watching war scenes and brutalisation of individuals. Not even places of worship were spared from the strafing of bombs and bullets. Civilised behaviour was thrown to the winds, as people were daily faced with the issues of food and survival.

Alozie I. Ikonne

The family compound of Ezeoha had large cocoa plantations on both sides. Actually, the cocoa was used as both cash crops and shade. During hot days, one would go into the cocoa farm to receive cool breeze and even meditation. The raging war kept attracting more displaced people who seemed to find the village of Umueke a safe haven.

Both the villagers and the displaced people who were living with them were shocked to notice the presence of soldiers from the land of Ala. Initially; people thought they came to conscript young men into the Army. But after about a week, the soldiers did not go away, everyone became worried.

Ezeoha's father's compound became the resting place of the soldiers. Initially, they were not more than twelve people who were patrolling the village and other adjoining villages. Later, they started sleeping under the cocoa plantation.

Information came that the twelfth division of the Army of Ala came under enemy attack. So they had to relocate to a more convenient place where they could hide their armoury. Before long, Ezeoha's compound had become a military barrack.

All manner of military hardware were increasingly packed under the cocoa plantation. The soldiers that used to visit had come to live at the village of Umueke, and the people must come to accept the facts of their current situation.

The early morning drills and the blowing of the trumpets were familiar scenes. Ezeoha would wake up to hear 'Corporal Gogo, fall in, and later, Corporal Gogo, fall out'. And someone with a jackboot would march out in military- style fashion and take the salute.

The presence of the military in the village introduced a new set of challenges for both the adults and children. Prior to their coming, issues and matters were settled by elders without force and rancour. Young men wooed young women into marriage relationships. But the presence of the soldiers introduced strange cultures of force and violence.

Young women were forcefully 'captured' as either wives or sex object. Young women were raped and violated against their will. The usual humility youths had towards elders were replaced with brash and arrogant dispositions. The village foundation that was anchored on respect for elders and the rule of law was thrown overboard by the soldiers who defined and decided how they would live in the village of Umueke.

Although Ezeoha's compound played hosts to the military, the father's yams and other valuables were not spared either. One major casualty of their presence was the domestic animals his father had. Every goat or sheep that missed its way to the barn was 'captured' by the soldiers and killed for dinner. That same approach was later extended to all the dogs and chicken in the village. Hungry soldiers from Ala, who slaughtered it for dinner one day forcefully, took Ezeoha's pet dog from his arms.

The few months the soldiers stayed in the village saw the decimation of the population of all domestic animals. By the time the war became hot around Umueke at the middle of 1969, one would need to diligently search to find any dog or fowl around the village. They were like hungry locusts released to feast on anything within their vicinity. Those soldiers seemed to be prosecuting the war at their own expense as even their own food was rationed.

As the war was coming to an end, everyone in the village came to the conclusion: war is not the route to settlement of disputes! Aside from the psychological trauma people were subjected to, its major toll was on the cultural and social orientation. Children who grow up under war situations are most likely to develop deviant and defiant attitudes later on in life.

As the ember months in Umueke were approaching, the usual end of the year celebrations was anticipated. But towards December 1969, rumours and stories started making the rounds that the people of Elu were having the upper hand as the war was progressing. Villages like Umueke and other parts of the nation of Ala were losing their military positions to the advancing soldiers of Elu.

Ezeoha and other children could hear shells of artillery pieces booming closer and closer. The greatest sign to the people of Umueke that the war was getting closer to their village was when the soldiers of Ala that were stationed at their village started moving some of their military wares and shifting towards the hinterland.

The people did not need to see another prophet to decipher that they too needed to start moving towards the hinterlands. Ezeoha's father had to take his few belongings and his entire family to begin his own journey as a 'refugee' to another village.

As Ezeoha and his family members were leaving his beloved village, he kept thinking about what the future held for him and other children who were of school age, but could not go because of war. With people from various parts of Ala nation moving towards other areas where bullets were less destructive, the picture was worrisome.

Men and women, carrying household items on their heads, and women clutching their children on their backs, the picture was most pathetic. People were crossing rivers, bridges and streams without having a clear-cut destination. Without food supplies and water, everyone was moving, expecting anything to happen.

The initial apprehension that Ezeoha and his village people faced started turning to hope of survival when they settled in another village called Ogbe for two weeks. His mother was able to cook soup for the family to enjoy a good meal for days.

Since the young men had gone into the bush to evade conscription into the army of Ala, the coast was then cleared for the invading troops of Elu who quickly took over the territories vacated by the retreating soldiers of Ala.

When it became obvious that no one could challenge the authority of the invading soldiers of Elu over the abuse of women especially young girls, an ingenious strategy was adopted to prevent soldiers from raping young women. Many young women had to resort to painting their faces with charcoal and sooth in order to look ugly. Rags and disused clothing materials were distributed to young women to wear so as to disguise their beauty.

Those women that were exceptionally beautiful had to add another trick to discourage the soldiers from 'capturing' them. They borrowed little children which they strapped on their backs, creating the impression that they were actually nursing mothers.

Some women on their own volition actually ran to stay with the soldiers. Because of the scarcity of foot wears, the soldiers gave to their girl friends a special kind of bathroom slippers usually referred to as 'red slippers'. It was so addressed because; the sole of the slippers was made of red colour. Possessing such slippers at that time was a sign that a lady was connected to the soldiers who seemed to throw their little weight around.

A lady that had any form of connections to the occupying soldiers of Elu was treated with some measure of apprehension. This was to avoid the lady reporting her adversaries to the soldiers which could earn severe punishment to the offender.

The air bombardment from the army of Elu was almost gone at this point, and people were just wondering what was really happening at the land of Ala. While the next line of action was being contemplated, information reached the refugees that the elders of Ala and Elu were meeting to settle the war situation. While people were trying to savour the news, the armies of Elu conducted air raids and strikes. This made

Ezeoha and his family members to move towards another town called Ulor.

It was at Ulor that soldiers of Ala started throwing their uniforms and weapons away, as they carried palm fronts. People were singing, dancing, and waving leaves and other items of fancy as they shouted: 'One Niger Area! One Niger Area!' At last, the war had ended and the nightmare was over, so they thought...

"Peace makers and negotiators can help end a conflict, but the greater challenge is how to manage the peace- time phase."

-Alozie Israel Ikonne

CHAPTER 4
END OF THE NIGHTMARE

That bright morning of 15 January 1970 saw the end of official hostilities between the country of Ala and their Elu brothers. Earlier in the morning, Ezeoha had gone into the bush to 'take cover' with some of the family members. Under the palm tree, Ezeoha could still see bullets flying across the shrubs and trees. Having been warned earlier never to stand up when bullets were flying, Ezeoha dutifully lay prostrate at the base of the palm tree.

A few hours later, information from a new person running into the bush to hide, revealed that some soldiers from the country of Ala who did not want to surrender were the reason for that morning's exchange of gun-fire between the soldiers of Elu and the resistant Ala fighters.

When it became obvious that the war had come to an end, the resistant Ala fighters threw in the towel, and removed their military uniforms. One of the retreating soldiers came around the bush where Ezeoha and others were taking refuge to ask for a civilian shirt.

The victorious troops of the Elu army soon mounted mega phones on their military vehicle announcing 'One Niger Area', One Niger Area'. They told every soldier to surrender and hand in their weapons, while those who were hiding in the bush were told to come out. That day was like another Christmas for the people of Ala.

Everyone who had gone to the bush to hide started coming out to enjoy the end of the nightmare that had plagued the people of Ala for about thirty months. With palm fronts in hand, and a ready mouth to shout 'One Niger Area' when asked by the soldiers of Elu nation, the journey back to the village of Umueke started in earnest.

Mothers strapped their children at the back, fathers carrying cooking utensils and other household items on their heads; different walk styles created scenery of despair and hope. While some people were rejoicing at the prospect of going back to their ancestral homes, others contemplated the grim realities of starting life afresh.

People moved in measured and calculated steps as the weak and elderly ones were assisted to make the homeward journey. Like the typical Israelites on their way out of Egypt, the mass of hurting, angry, lonely and tired legs was a pitiable sight to behold. One consoling fact though, was that the people were going home at last.

It took four days for Ezeoha and his village people to make the journey back home to Umueke. Though the journey of over 80 miles was made on foot, the damaged roads and bridges presented their own challenges. The roads were littered with decomposing bodies of dead soldiers and civilians who died in the course of the war.

Along the route to Umueke, at a point, Ezeoha and his people had to cross a big river on wooden canoe because the bridge was blown up in the course of the war. Even the route through the river was mined with explosives.

Celebrating the safe departure from the very point of death called for thanksgiving and prayers for Ezeoha and his family members. As Ezeoha and his parents' waited for other family members to cross the Omi River, using wooden canoes on the dirty banks of the river, something strange happened. Every person that passed through the small bush road that led to the river was subjected to intense security search by the victorious soldiers of the army of Elu.

Suddenly, there was a loud bang at the check point. Inquisitive children who had gone for sightseeing were forced to retreat and hang around their mothers. Information filtered that someone had been shot dead by the Elu soldiers, who assumed that the young man was an ex-Ala soldier who had just surrendered. Ezeoha could not wait to see for himself the gory sight of a lifeless body that was killed by a trigger-happy soldier, using his Mark IV gun.

When Ezeoha came back to the spot where his mother was staying, every manner of story started flying around as the reason why the soldiers were killing people. Some people said that the soldiers were searching for weapons and other implements of war. At this disclosure, everyone who had a knife threw them away. Mothers frantically searched their luggage and anything that could incriminate them or their children before the fierce looking soldiers.

The long wait at the bank paid off as Ezeoha and his entire family members were ready to commence their journey towards Umueke. As they got to the checkpoint, every person was searched as this was the normal routine. But when the older brother of Ezeoha named Ome, stood before the soldiers, one of them asked him whether he was once a soldier. The young man answered that he had never been one.

As they looked at his tattered dress, one of the soldiers spotted a mark on his chest. The other soldier watching, shouted 'kill him, he is an enemy'. The boy cried out that he was not a soldier, but sustained a wound on the chest when he was cutting down a bamboo tree. Another soldier that was watching the drama pleaded with his fellows to find out the truth about the boy.

When a little argument ensued between the two soldiers over the propriety of killing a young boy, a third person suggested that they should call the mother of Ome. When the mother of Ome came around, she knelt down at the feet of the trigger-happy soldier who seemed to relish killing people even when the war was over. Because the mother of Ome was an illiterate woman who could not speak English, and the soldier could not understand her native language, the woman's pleading sounded theatrical to the soldiers who soft-pedalled and gave a little grinning.

At this point, the mother of Ome and their village people started another round of pleading that Ome was never a soldier. The mark on his chest was sustained when they went to the farm to cut down some bamboo trees, and he was cut on the chest. The father of Ome finally confirmed that his son was not an ex soldier. On the testimony of Ome's father, he was released to go with other family members on their onward journey home.

It was therefore a thing of joy for Ezeoha and his family members to return to his beloved village one Friday afternoon. On setting his feet on his compound, Ezeoha's father raised his hands in supplication to God for sparing the life of all members of the family without anyone dying. After the initial surprise at the devastation done to buildings and the environment, everyone went into clean up exercise. With some doors broken and bullet holes all over the buildings, the gory picture of war was then evident.

It took about one month for most villagers to finally return to their homes. Those that arrived earlier helped themselves with whatever they could find in the village. In a village where it was a taboo to steal or pilfer things, people found out that pot, bicycles and other properties that were left behind had all been stolen. Some people had their houses burnt, while soldiers and natives in search of valuables broke into not a few doors.

The war ended during the early months of the year, which were farming months. People had started picking the pieces of their lives together again. Ezeoha's father cleared the surrounding lands around their compound in preparation for planting crops. A strange incidence that had never occurred in the village of Umueke happened the day his father set the bush on fire.

Live ammunition the occupying soldiers left in his compound started to explode as soon as they came in contact with fire. Initially, there was a mild drama, as no one knew where the bullets would explode the next time. Ezeoha and his father had to run away from the farm while the bullets kept exploding on end. By the grace of God, no one was hurt.

The following year after the war, Ezeoha's father decided to farm the other section of his vast backyard farm. The usual method of clearing and subsequent bush burning was carried out. But this time around, the consequences of bush burning around military settlement were almost fatal. One of the bunkers used by the soldiers of Ala while they stayed in Umueke had some explosives.

The fire made some of the grenades to explode. It was by an act of divine intervention that no one was eventually killed when the devises exploded. Eventually, the hurdles placed on the path of that year's farming season was overcome by the determination of the people to take their destiny in their hands. Since the needed seed for planting was virtually absent, people used ingenious means to develop seedlings.

Trying to survive after a war situation proved to everyone in Umueke that lost ground is difficult to recover. Peace makers and negotiators can help end a conflict, but the greater challenge is how to manage the peace- time phase.

With virtually every infrastructure destroyed or non-functioning, life became unbearable and the social cohesion that hitherto existed started giving way to individual survival.

Self interest and personal advancement took the centre stage. The people of Umueke and indeed the entire nation of Ala had come to grapple with a new phenomenon: - personal survival as against corporate survival. But how far could they go?

'No one is born a criminal, the society makes one so. The surest way to either reduce or minimise crime, is to change the prevailing social conditions'.

- Dr Kwameh Nkurumah of Ghana

CHAPTER 5

NEW STRENGTH, NEW COURAGE AND DASHED HOPES

It was a glorious moment for the people of Elu and Ala when the war between them had finally ended on the basis of 'no victor, no vanquished'. The broken bridges and other artificial barriers that for over thirty months separated brothers and friends were finally over. Travel restrictions and other internal policies that made it difficult for the people of Elu and Ala to socialise were completely removed.

In the euphoria of victory, and in the spirit of reconciliation, the government of the now united Niger Area announced a policy package known as the three Rs. The three Rs represent Reconciliation, Reconstruction and Rehabilitation. This policy was more like the Marshal Plan for Europe after the devastating Second World War.

While the Marshal Plan for Europe succeeded to a great extent in rebuilding Europe, the 3R policy of the Niger Area was a practical example of policy summersault and failure. There was therefore neither true reconciliation, nor reconstruction and rehabilitation.

When the people of Ala region waited for the promised help in rehabilitating infrastructure in their devastated land was no more than mere slogan, there was total disillusionment especially on the part of the youths. Having waited in vain for the new lease of life, which never materialised, there was massive exodus of young people to other parts of the re-united nation where opportunities abound.

With little or no opportunities around, coupled with psychological defeat, hundreds of thousands of young men and women literarily migrated from the land of Ala, which incidentally was the theatre of war to other parts of the country. The social consequences of migration were soon to be felt.

There was cross-cultural fertilization of ideas. A kind of hybrid culture and ethos emerged. Since there was no deliberate effort to lay ground rules for social engagement, what became of the city life was competitive spirit as opposed to complementary efforts.

Since there was no defined social contract between the various ethnic groups that came to have a piece of the national cake, ethnic and tribal cleavages became the norm, as individuals did not care about what happens to the common wealth. What mattered most was what any and everyone could get out of living together in a modern city.

Sharing of the few opportunities that existed at the centre of government had its own peculiar challenges. Since some parts of the new Niger Area had already lost some grounds as a result of where they fought the war, those who felt not favoured in the allocation of resources and socio-economic patronage started devising means of survival in a competitive setting.

According to the words of the late Ghanaian sage, Dr Kwame Nkurumah: 'No one is born a criminal, the society makes one so. The surest way to either reduce or minimise crime, is to change the prevailing social conditions'. One of the most pronounced consequences of the civil war was the introduction of the culture of violence.

Secondly, the war destroyed the original societal mechanism of conflict resolution. With dashed hopes and uncertain future, majority of young men and women became social deviants. Armed robbery, assassinations and lawlessness became entrenched. The theory of might is right, replaced the age long Golden Rule of 'do unto others as you would have them do unto you'.

Many youths whose lives were temporarily demobilised during the war were in a hurry to catch up with their counter parts on the other side of the divide. Since resources were barely enough to go round, a feeling of marginalisation developed among the people of Ala. They must either have a breakthrough or a break down. But how far could they go?

'When a child goes on the wrong errand, that child would be made to repeat the journey'

- (African Proverb)

CHAPTER 6

THE RIGHT ROAD THAT WAS NEVER TAKEN

The end of the civil war in the Niger Area brought to the fore the basic issue of human development. After the combatants had sheathed their swords, and the common people had received the bitter effects of civil unrest, one major issue became pronounced: society develops according to foundational structures on her path of growth.

One may tell a blind person that there is no oil in a soup. But it would be difficult to convince the blind person that there is no pepper in the soup when obviously the fellow is feeling the effects of pepper.

Everyone who witnessed the war saw the urgent need to reorganize the Niger Area after a structure that would enable the citizens to contribute their own quota in the development of the country. So many pronouncements; albeit emotional and spontaneous, were made as to the need to urgently put the country on the path of development again.

But unfortunately, as in all human experience, the road that is least travelled sometimes turns out to be the one that holds the compass for a safe journey. Effort was made to reconstruct in the land of Ala, although the attempt was too feeble to make a lasting impact. However, it was unfortunate that no attempt was made to 'reconstruct' the psyche of the people in terms of human capacity development.

The effect of this oversight is that there arose a generation of young men and women on both sides that fought the war in Elu and Ala, who

46

have never been taught what patriotism and nationalism means. The result is that some secret misgivings and suspicion still pervade all aspects of the socio-political interaction between the peoples of Elu and Ala. The clear absence of a defined national ethos and the lack of the will power to demand from the citizens, in clear terms, what should be the attitude of all citizens towards one another have hampered national cohesion.

Nations that have developed passed through the process of education. This type of education has a philosophy behind it. One could use education as a tool for human development or vice versa. At the end of the hostilities between the people of Elu and Ala, undue emphasis was placed on rebuilding physical infrastructure, without any commensurate effort to re-orientate the people on both sides of the divide, the need to live in harmony with one another.

The various regions were further split into smaller units called States. People, who once belonged to one Region, suddenly discovered that they no longer belong together, but have been shared into different States. Everyone gradually moved away from 'Regions' to 'States'. Every document began to bear the word 'state of origin'. The deliberate policy of putting people into compartments of States brought its own challenge of nation building. Educational opportunities, employment, privileges and activities of governance became influenced by the person's State of Origin.

Anyone who has ever worked on iron knows that the best time to bend a metal is when it is hot. When the steel is cooled, it would require a considerable amount of force and pressure to bend it. This analogy is what happened at the end of the civil war between the people of Elu and Ala. The civil war ended with bitter memories as people on both sides of the conflict lost their dear ones.

Almost everyone at the end of the hostilities would listen to anybody who seemed to have the panacea for avoiding future conflicts. With the hurting people trading blames on each other, anything that would make for permanent peace would be most welcome. But then, expectations are not always realized!

BLAME NOT THE CHILD

The leadership of the Niger Area lost one of the best moments in history to forge a united and prosperous nation. Instead of closing the roads that led to the civil war, they left them wide open and even opened other roads of similar destination. The civil war became a revolution without a defined agenda.

In other climes, wars redefine people and their orientation. But in the case of the Niger Area, there was no sustained effort to blend the diversities of the people into a single national driving force. The old mantra 'one nation, one destiny' was often repeated, but the practice was more in the breach than deeds.

The result was recourse to the old, archaic systems and methods that have hindered the potentials of the diverse groups from taking their deserved places among the progressive people of the earth. All over the world, education has always been a tool for human capacity development and social engineering. That is why all revolutionaries use education as a tool of communicating what they want their followers to assimilate.

Alozie I. Ikonne

The human nature is designed to follow and act on what is constantly presented before him or her. What people see, hear and speak eventually affects their lives. That is why educationists use the best curriculum when fashioning out ways of training children right from infancy.

One major mistake the leaders of the Niger Area made after the civil war was the inability to fuse the various ethnic nationalities into a nation state. There was no 'guiding document' that taught people the values of patriotism and infuse national consciousness among the ethnic nationalities. The consequence of this was the development of young people whose allegiance was neither here nor there. The educational curriculum did not help matters as the system encouraged differential development between the people of Elu and Ala.

In Ala land, there was emphasis on full western education. While in the land of Elu, there was a mixture of western education with religious bias. The result of this system became evident in the wider context of national educational development. The differential levels of learning created an educational dichotomy between the people of Elu and Ala. In effect, religion has polarized the people of Elu and Ala; as those with religious bias see the nation from the angle of their religious leanings.

The post war generation of the Niger Area has grown to grapple with a new challenge which their founding fathers never had: a nation torn apart along religious lines. Ezeoha's generation has seen more sectarian violence, religious riots than his father's. All major religions preach peace, tolerance and the need to be one's brother's keeper.

It is an irony today that crisis of phenomenal proportions, which have their roots in wrong religious education have wrecked havoc on the people and infrastructure in the Niger Area. People with the intention to maim, destroy and frustrate their country men and women; teach things that destabilize and erode national unity.

Are we right to blame a child who has never seen his educators and religious teachers live out what they teach and preach. Do we really have the right to blame children who have been brainwashed into thinking that their own religious ways are superior to the others, and as such, they have a right to maim or even destroy anyone who disagrees with them.

Would it not have been more honourable to let a child know, from the cradle that humanity has various differences? Would it not be better to let children know that the beauty of the world today is variety of people, lands and colours? How would the earth be a better place if all people have one face, colour, land and houses?

One tragic loss that befell the Niger Area after the civil war was the momentum of building a brand new nation. What the leadership should have done after the cessation of hostilities was to isolate the various factors that have worked against national cohesion, call a summit of the various nationalities to a round table conference where each group would discuss and agree on what should be the national priority.

But this was never done. Instead, various people were merely asked to go and develop their areas without a national model or working document. The result today is a nation where one side is developing, and another side is retarding in all parameters of growth. Where there is abject poverty in the midst of plenty is a paradox. Where there is scarcity, in spite of generous natural endowment is still a big puzzle.

When people believe, rightly or wrongly that the reason for their manifest backwardness and frustration, is the presence of other people groups outside their tribal homeland, something is fundamentally wrong. This faulty perception has generated social fear and insecurity, such that there is reasonable suspicion between 'indigenes' and 'settler elements' in all parts of the Niger Area.

A nation can have real unity and cohesion as exemplified during the time when the national football team is playing another country. At such periods, everyone talks and stays together and enjoy each other's company. If football could temporarily unite a country, and then, something could still be done to cement the unity of the various people groups for the job of building a nation of our dreams.

When a product is not selling well, good marketers rebrand it. The rebranding process eliminates the factors that hinder sales, and highlight the things that make the product desirable and necessary. The Niger Area is a brand, and majority of her people do not feel that it is selling very well. There is therefore the need for the people to rebrand it. Every rebranding involves identifying key areas that have given problems, eliminating them and replacing them with better options that can fly.

The Niger Area is a project that needs redesigning. A major component of the designing process is to ask the various people groups to bring their finest ideas, put those ideas into a 'national pot', stir that pot and let the contents blend. What eventually comes out of that 'pot' will be the 'new brand' which every citizen would be asked to wear and promote.

There is an African saying that 'when a child goes on the wrong errand, that child would be made to repeat the journey'. The Niger Area like a child; had repeatedly gone on the wrong way in creating a nation that could withstand the vagaries of modern nationhood. She has to repeat the journey, even if it is belated to right what was done wrong at her foundation.

BLAME NOT THE CHILD

The people of the Niger Area have travelled very far on the wrong road to national cohesion and development. There is an urgent need for the present generation to go back to the right road which was never taken. Only the right road leads to the right destination, and this path is both necessary and desirable for the people to develop truly in infrastructure and in her human capacity indices.

"Any community that does not want someone to rise as a leader will always remain at the bottom of achievement and development."

-Alozie Israel Ikonne

CHAPTER 7
THE STRUGGLE
FOR THE CAKE

T he strength of any society is determined by its foundational philosophy and social contract. When the basis of union and cooperation are not defined, every other thing tends to represent what was not originally intended.

One of the fundamental flaws that have dogged the history of Niger Area is the near absence of what each group in the union ought to bring to the table, and by implication, what every group ought to contribute to the common purse.

This obvious omission from the beginning has created a feeling of suspicion among the various components of the union. One word that has taken a larger than life meaning in the Niger Area project is marginalisation. From the North to the South, and East to the West, everyone is marginalized.

In every appointment made, someone is marginalized. Every road that is constructed, schools that are built, airports that are sited, population and census figures, and above all, infrastructures development, has someone down the line who is shouting marginalisation!

The people of Ala after the civil war felt that they have been marginalized by reason of infrastructural decay and lack of economic empowerment. The feeling that the civil war has delayed them from catching up with the rest of the country also created a peculiar social problem among the people. The crab theory is a graphic illustration of the social problem.

BLAME NOT THE CHILD

The crab is a sea creature with a hard shell, eight legs and two pincers (these are curved and pointed arms for catching and holding things). They usually move sideways on land especially on swamp. Because the crab has pincers, it is usually difficult to hold it with the bare hand. When they are caught, they are placed into basins with some water.

One discovery that has been made is that no matter the quantity of crabs in a particular basin, it is always difficult for any of them to escape. The reason they do not run away is because each crab is a hindrance to one another. The ones on top would like to remain on top, but the ones below will do anything to make sure that those on top are pulled down.

Anyone down the basin would like to come up in an escape bid, but others around will use their pincers to pull down the ones that try to rise up. In this way, the entire crab end up staying put in the basin. None of them is greater than the other. They just hang around the same place without making appreciable movement. This is the way those that know how to handle crab keep them busy in a place without any progressive movement.

One major effect of the crab theory is that they enter the basin with their limbs intact, but eventually leave with broken limbs. By pulling and tearing at each other, many limbs are lost in the process. Any community that does not want someone to rise as a leader will always remain at the bottom of achievement and development.

This principle is applicable whether at the animal level or human level. If the crabs are wise enough to allow some of their colleagues to escape from the basin, it would be possible for those who have escaped to help their friends inside to come out to safety.

The people of Ala after the war went in different directions to look for the means of survival. While the rest of the people in the Niger Area seemed to know what they really wanted, their counterparts in Ala were busy looking for anything that would be personally beneficial to them and their immediate families. They were in every nook and cranny of the re-united country doing just anything to get money and survive.

The original cooperative spirit that was the foundation of their socio-cultural life was replaced with the individualistic spirit. Like the crab, any person from Ala who happens to get a portion or position from the Central Government was never celebrated. Instead of helping that person to consolidate, the very brothers and sisters would be the ones that would be used by other tribes to pull them down.

In any society where there is inequality and deep injustice, the struggle for the central cake (national) is always intense. The people groups that are wise fight collectively for their own share of the cake. But those who are not wise fight for individual crumps that fall from the masters' table.

Like all projects and enterprises, it is a common axiom that lost ground is always not easy to recover. If the people of Ala were aware of the dangers of one mortgaging his or her future for mere empty promises of a future Eldorado, they would be more circumspect in conducting their affairs.

To survive in the Niger Area project, the people of Ala need to re-engineer their self-help spirit and stop living the selfish lifestyle that has become their trademarks. The outcome of the lifestyles of individual members of a society is tied to the very structure of the society.

A country like the Niger Area is like a polygamous family with the centre playing the role of a father, and individual components of the nation, acting as the children from various mothers. Usually in a polygamous family, one trait that is very pronounced is the spirit of competition and favouritism.

Obviously the favoured wife and her children would most likely corner the best things in the house. This often leads to infighting and skirmishes. When children from the wife who is not favoured, see that they stand no chance of getting anything, some resort to rebellion and living as outlaws.

A nation that encourages her citizens to depend on the centre, for all their supplies, will sooner than later, be reduced to a theatre of conflicts. When children learn that hard work and merit do not advance any person beyond the level of an errand boy, they will ultimately resort to living by self-help.

Societies and nations that do not direct the focus and efforts of her citizen towards productive ventures, but rather encourage them to wait for rations from a central purse are doomed already.

No nation will ever advance beyond the productive capacities of her citizens. A nation like Niger Area where her people from the East, West, North and South are encouraged to have their knives ready to cut their own share of the national cake will continue to be a consumer nation, without the means of productive capacities.

A situation where the issue is how to share the natural cake like oil, which no one contributed to its presence under the soil, will take the nation nowhere. Real and strong nations are those that challenge their people groups to use their minds and brains to solve problems of humanity, thereby attracting prosperity to their people.

An atmosphere where youths do not see demonstrative actions towards real national development, but the old worn- out tale of how to share the national cake and the icing thereof, will produce delinquent and perverse youths who do not live for anything worthwhile. When young ones do not have real role models, except the ones that were artificially created, then the future looks bleak.

A society that has no real regard for honesty and hard work, but glorifies pimps and scoundrels with national honours has killed the spirit of nobility. When a system permits the acquisition of wealth without labour, then the path of lawlessness is clearly entrenched.

One fact of life is that bad money in any environment generates discord and evils. A society that has no defined system of rising through the social and corporate ladder will only succeed in enthroning mediocrity over and above excellence. Merit suffers at the altar of nepotism.

In life, every restoration begins at the point of departure. Therefore the need to re-define our national ethos and values is the sine qua non for our nation to begin the journey of greatness. These indeed we must do now!

"A nation that encourages her citizens to depend on the centre, for all their supplies, will sooner than later, be reduced to a theatre of conflicts."

-Alozie Israel Ikonne

CHAPTER 8

THE PYRAMID AND THE CONE: WHICH OPTIONS?

The end of the civil war posed some fresh problems for the Niger Area. The component units suffered one form of challenge or the other. For instance, at the end of the war, everyone from the land of Ala that deposited money into any bank had his or her deposit reduced to a flat amount of twenty pounds sterling.

That means that if you had four hundred thousand pounds, before the war, you would only be entitled to a mere twenty pounds just because you happen to come from the land of Ala.

In nations that are prone to earthquakes, and indeed all places that experience earth movements, one major event that keeps people on the toes, is the aftershock effect. It is just like a child who had once been bitten by a snake that easily runs at the mere presence of a lizard's head.

In life, hidden fears play significant roles in determining where people end up on the journey to destiny. Therefore, many practitioners of psychology try to allay the hidden fears of their clients if they must help them out of any problems.

One major effect of the war and prolonged military rule is the adjustment of the rule of engagement for the component units of the Niger Area project. Whereas at the foundation of the structure, the founding fathers envisaged a country where each component unit would develop at its own pace, the reverse became the case.

The original pyramid structure where each base was supposed to be strong and help out the top (Central Government) was replaced with a cone that is carrying the big bases. Because the cone has a shallow foundation, spinning dangerously on the pinnacle, its weight is unable to support the bases, and that is why the country is perennially shaky.

The greatest task the leaders of the Niger Area have faced over the years is how to stabilize the cone from tripping, and that is the tragedy of the nation. When the foundation is weak and leaders devote the most important times of constructive and productive thinking to making the structure stabilize, before they know it, nothing is achieved in terms of real statecraft.

Any structure where the Architect spends the entire allotted time of executing a project in redesigning, and adjustment of the original plan, will never take off from the ground level. The nightmare of the Niger Area today is that similar nations and countries that took off at the same time with the country; are today structurally defined, organized to a large extent, and functional nations.

Ours is a classic illustration of a nation in perennial experimentation. Every new leader starts with the often worn out cliché 'we are in a learning process'. A student that never learns to graduate is a drain on the resources of the parents as well as the state.

Only a few institutions can afford the luxury of having professional students all the time. The joy of academics is having a time of matriculation and also a time of graduation. That is what makes the cycle and rhythm complete.

The Niger Area project must definitely seek to adopt new strategies if it intends to recon among nations that are serious about development. The nation for almost five decades has been standing on the cone, carrying the burden of the bases. The entire bases run to the apex of the cone every month for their sustenance.

A situation whereby all component units of a country depend on the central government for virtually everything they do is certainly unwieldy. It is only in the Niger Area where every traditional ruler, politician, praise singer, charlatan, hustlers etc. devote precious man hours to go and pay homage and courtesy calls on the head of government.

Anyone who has the luck of becoming the Head of State, spends more than two-thirds of the days in any given year, welcoming a retinue of traditional rulers, town union executives, women association from zone A, men's association from zone C, market union from zone E, and religious leaders from zone F, and of course different political interests that want to be relevant.

The time wasted in talking and interacting with these callers, hardly gives the leadership the needed focus and concentration on managing the complex socio-cultural and economic problems of the nation.

The major tragedy of building a nation on the cone concept, instead of the base; is that the head of government becomes a social prisoner, who has to make sure that he serves all the centripetal and centrifugal forces that tug and pull at the very soul of good governance. The foundational concept of unity in diversity must be given the right climate to flourish. What is killing the Niger Area today is the replacement of the concept of 'unity in diversity', with monolithic unity.

It is often said that variety is the spice of life. A country where various talents and endowments are not recognised, unless they are first blended together in the national pot, thereby destroying individualism and unique traits, may not access the benefits of diversity.

A situation where what part A, discovers to be the panacea for a social problem is not accepted, unless someone from part B discovers the same, then it would be difficult to arrive at the Promised Land for such a nation.

No nation can ever develop when one part is held down from moving forward unless the other parts catch up with each other. Even nature did not make all the surfaces of the earth to be equal. The reason why this earth is beautiful today is because of the varying landscapes and seas that dot the various portions of the earth's surface.

If God in His wisdom could allow stratified development on the surface of the earth, then let the people and leadership of the Niger Area allow various endowments of the different segments of the nation to find expression, without the fear that someone would destroy the unity of the nation, which some people revere and also consider sacrosanct.

The task before the peoples of the Niger Area today is, whether to build a nation of one centrally strong point, or empower the various units of the component parts to be strong, and therefore avoid the pull to the centre. This pull to the centre is the root cause of all the problems confronting the emergence of a virile, strong and powerful nation that all citizens would be proud of. Let men of goodwill arise, and do this task!

"The greed of man is as deep as the ocean. It should not be left unchecked."

-Alozie Israel Ikonne

CHAPTER 9

OUT OF THE ASHES..

The scramble for survival and the attendant cutthroat antics of the post war children of the Niger Area has presented another dimension to the already hydra-headed problems of the place. Ezeoha and the other children from the land of Ala that survived the war have all grown up into adulthood. The Holy book says 'The fathers have eaten sour grapes, and the children's teeth are set on edge (Ezekiel 18:2)'.

Alozie I. Ikonne

The same problems that confronted the elders of the country of the Niger Area, that led to the civil war are still the challenges faced by the generation of Ezeoha. After many years of pontifications, the leopard has refused to change its spot.

Insensitivity to the feelings of others, ethnicity, structures and systems that deliberately stifle other people's aspirations and goals, inability to differentiate between creativity and competition among so many other factors, are the issues that have dogged our collective aspirations.

The most pressing problem and challenge that has faced the nation is the tendency of the leaders to look the other way when they should sit down and call a spade a spade. Abdication of one's responsibilities as a leader will never correct structural imbalances within the system.

History teaches that one of the remote causes of the American War of Independence was taxation without representation. The British Government was collecting taxes and levies from citizens who escaped persecution to the United States.

While they were forcing them to pay taxes to the British Government, they had no representation at the British Parliament. The deprived people felt that it was unfair to collect taxes without fulfilling the necessary obligations.

The implication of this scenario is that in any given society, there are foundational, irreducible minimum, which serve as the benchmark for the social contract between people groups in any given region. Any society that has no defined ethos or creed for co-habitation will eventually create loopholes for the component units to become lawless.

The founding fathers of the Niger Area in their wisdom, proposed a Federal System of administration, which also recognised that each component unit of the federation has the inalienable right to self-development.

One of the key foundational agreements, between the federating units was the issue of human development, natural resource sharing and management.

The greed of man is as deep as the ocean. It should not be left unchecked. If there were no framework for regulating and sharing resources that accrue to the nation, those who were privileged to control the apparatus of statecraft would corner all to their areas.

When public service is used as a means to an end, and when endemic and systemic corruption is seen as a normal thing, then the society is already doomed to confusion.

The greatest challenge today facing the people of the Niger Area is how to create a nation and society where truth and equity reign supreme.

Any form of injustice is an attack on justice itself. If the leaders remember and recognise that the greatest service they could do their nation and peoples, is to rule with fairness and equity, to all at any given time, then the society is on its way to fulfilling the purpose of creating a state.

A socio-political structure that encourages people to reap where they did not sow; and denies others the opportunity of reaping where they sowed, would sooner than later nurture social deviants.

When youths watch the glorification of ill-gotten wealth and materialism as the dividends of government service, what do you expect them to imbibe?

BLAME NOT THE CHILD

When a child sees the father sign a contract with the government, collect mobilization money, and end up in a five-star hotel with women of easy virtue, without doing the contract, and yet nobody calls the felon to account, what do you expect that child to do? When a child sees that the highest National Honours of his or her country are bestowed on thieves and dupes, what do you expect the role model to be?

A society where many leaders are remembered when they leave office, not by their developmental strides, but by the sheer amount of cash they were able to steal from the public till, and the degree of pain and misery they were able to inflict upon their fellow citizens, is already doomed to failure.

In other climes, and societies where things are done the right way, people who are true role models, are measured by the amount of smiles they were able to put on the faces of their country men and women. Those who add value to life and society, by improving the living conditions of their people are the ones who ought to be celebrated.

People, whose legacy after public office is the number of cars, chains of houses and numerous concubines they acquired while in office, do not deserve to be glorified, and ought to be publicly labelled and addressed by what they represent. A society that fails to accord recognition to men and women who play by the rules, but prefers to celebrate people of questionable characters certainly has no enviable future.

Any society that closes the main road to her young ones has automatically compelled them to resort to bush tracts. When a child is denied good parental upbringing and sound education, because those whose primary responsibilities to raise him or her, fail in their God-ordained assignments, how would you blame the child?

A child that is inundated daily with pictures and words that depict adults cutting corners to make it in life, what future has that child? A child, whose genuine educational pursuit is frustrated because of his or her tribal and religious inclination, may not be quick to play the patriotic card.

Would you blame a child who is deliberately held down from moving forward in life on account of whether he comes from educational advantaged or disadvantaged zones?

Would you blame a child, who is daily suffused with vain religious talk without seeing the numerous adherents live a simple life of truth and humility? Should we blame a child who sees majority of his countrymen and women stand the truth on its head in both private and public life?

Are we right to blame the child who is neglected by the very society he or she is born into, and yet we expect them to be patriotic in thinking and deeds? Would you blame the child who sees crude oil pipes drilled from his father's backyard, and sold; and the proceeds are used to develop other places, without the slightest consideration for his environment and needs?

Every leader that has ever mounted the saddle in the Niger Area project always begins with this mantra: "to clean the rot on the table". Unfortunately, by the time the new Messiah has finished his own tenure, what began as a rot, would have turned into a huge mountain of stench and filth that would eventually envelope and cover the entire country.

Alozie I. Ikonne

When government is run on profligacy, when the cost of keeping government officials is far greater than the amount reserved for real development, when the dividends of good governance are lacking, would you blame the child? When adults come to the market square and dance naked, would you penalise the child for watching to satisfy his eyes with the grotesque figures before him?

It is my considered opinion that the single most vicious power attacking the Niger Area project is the demon of materialism. After this, the first cousin, called disorder follows in that ranking. These sprits must be exorcised in all of us without exception, before our environmental clean up campaigns begin to bear the desired fruit.

Any attempt to ignore heart clean up would amount to scratching the surface without touching the interior.

When fathers, teachers, clerics, uncles and aunts, take our responsibilities in setting and living the right ways, then we would not contend with the troubles of blaming our future generations for not following the right paths.

BLAME NOT THE CHILD

Children live what they see. We have the divine mandate to show the right ways for our children to follow. This God-ordained duty and responsibility we must discharge faithfully.

Many nations have been raised out of the ashes of war to create modern, progressive and equitable states where the citizens are proud to flaunt their national identity. The ashes of war have been used as foundation stones to purify and reorganise society. It has always taken resolute commitment and steadfastness to turn things around.

Unfortunately, in the case of the Niger Area, the lessons of war seem to have been lost on the leaders who constantly and consistently stoke the embers of hatred and ethnic cleavages in the course of organising an enduring society.

History teaches that history has taught men nothing. If this present generation of leaders fail to make lasting marks in the area of paradigm shift from uncoordinated to coordinated leadership; then the future is bleak for the younger generation.

Every enduring society is built by men and women of goodwill. If they fail to rise up or are intimidated to retreat and retire; and then the society is worse off for it. The greatest tragedy that would befall the Niger Area after the unfortunate civil war is for men and women of goodwill to do nothing when the foundations of the nation are threatened. To go and hibernate when one's voice and contributions are required is to kill the seed that would produce our expected harvest.

The nation today needs moral and spiritual realignment to save the present and future generations. May God help us to purge and cleanse our rotten hearts, so that the future generation shall grow up without the perversions of our present foibles?